Timepieces

by Glenda Allen Chatham

6. 3. 14

May you always
use your time for
Him.

Glenda

Ps. 139

Illustrations by
Wendy Burchette

Timepieces

Copyright © 1998
Glenda Allen Chatham
First Printing 1998 (500 copies)

Cover: by Jon and Wendy Burchette

Library of Congress Catalog Card Number: 98-92656
ISBN: 978-1-57502-766-1

Printed in the USA by

MORRIS PUBLISHING

3212 East Highway 30 • Kearney, NE 68847 • 1-800-650-7888

Dedication

This book is dedicated to my husband,
Fred,
Who encourages me and loves me,
to my parents who gave me a Christian home,
and to Christian leaders who helped guide me during
my youth.

Love,
Glenda

Special thanks....
to my niece Wendy Burchette and her husband
Jon, for their dedication in helping me prepare my
book.

Contents

Timepieces

Years have a way of passing.
There have been many pieces of time.
I've been given a wonderful family
And many mountains to climb.

As I pass through this world,
Lord, I want to do my part.
I want to make the right impressions,
Find Your purpose and make my mark.

Lord, help me seek Your way;
Not go out on my own.
May You be pleased with me,
And my timepieces You have loaned.

Back In Time

I grew up in a mill village,
When life was very slow.
On Saturday
I went to the picture show.

My daddy worked
In the cotton mill.
People had time to listen
To the whippoorwill.

After work my daddy would go
To the park and play ball.
My mother and I watched him
Instead of going to a mall.

You didn't live in fear
And have to lock your door.
You could enjoy an ice cream
At the town's drug store.

A beggar felt free
To ask for something to eat,
Without being treated
Like some deadbeat.

Our rooms had fireplaces
And scuttles of coal.
I even had a goldfish
In a fishbowl.

You could walk to town
Or ride the bus for a nickel.
I remember when I got
My one and only bicycle.

2

The company store
Had a delivery man.
The children played a street game
Called "Kick the Can."

I liked to jump rope;
I jumped double dutch.
I made my own paper dolls
And liked to read very much.

It was fun making syrup candy
And playing Old Maid.
We would make our own popsicles
Out of grape Kool Aid.

I liked to read comic books,
And play Monopoly.
My friends and I would
Sing "Sixteen Tons" a little off key.

My saddle oxford shoes
Were quite in style.
The operator said, "Number please,"
Instead of telephones having buttons or dials.

It might be fun to visit
Back in time
And get to know each other
By sharing a party line.

But I don't wish
To relive my life;
I would just like to slow down
And have less strife.

Today is a beginning
All fresh and new.
I hope I can make a difference
In all that I do.

Roots Of A Village

The roots of a village
Are firmly fixed.
They draw you back
From the world's conflicts.

A warm hug from someone
Who never left,
Gives you a peace and rest
To be yourself.

There you can remember
A more simple time
And may even hear
An old church chime.

It's good to visit
Your village roots
And let the outside
World go mute.

Mill Village School

The mill village school wasn't a one-room schoolhouse,
But it was different from today.
There was one class for each grade of children.
A Bible story was read, and the students prayed.

If students were punished at school
For doing something wrong,
They knew their parents would work with the teachers
And had that to deal with all day long.

The daddies worked in the cotton mill;
Sometimes the mothers too,
But there was always someone home
When the kids came in from school.

The mill village school wasn't perfect.
There was some good and some bad going on;
But the roots planted in that old school
Are still deep and strong.

The Old School Gym

The old school gym
Wasn't just for ball.
It was more of a center
Used by all.

In May we had a Maypole
And a king and queen.
I was honored and crowned,
When I was near thirteen.

There was an auction to raise money
When we had box suppers.
There was lots of laughter.
It was a real picker-upper.

At the Halloween parties
I wished I could have been a mouseketeer.
I wore the same costume
My mother let out year after year.

I miss that old gym.
It burned down long ago;
But I still have my memories.
They keep my heart aglow.

Sounds Of A Train

I used to lie in bed and listen
To the train go down the track.
Some said it was a lonely sound,
But I liked how it kept coming back.

I would count the cars
As I waited to cross to the other side.
I wondered who the people were
In the seats that were occupied.

Outside our small village
Was farm land, mile after mile.
You might see an old country church
Every once in a while.

People in the village didn't
Usually go very far.
Every so often you might see
A hobo hop a boxcar.

It was nice living close
To a railroad track
And listening to the sounds
After you hit the sack.

First Day Of May

Back in the forties,
On the first day of May,
I could finally go barefoot.
My mother said "Okay."

It mattered not the weather,
Whether cold or hot;
Up until then my mother
Said that I could not.

I also shed my undershirt
With the little pink bow
And put on a dress
Made of calico.

It was always nice
When it was spring.
I dreamed of the day,
I would wear a class ring.

It was neat to hear
The ice cream man ring his bell.
All the neighborhood children
Would let out a yell.

My friends and I would
Skate down the sidewalk,
Play movie star hopscotch,
Giggle, and girl talk.

The kid on the corner
Had a lemonade stand;
While his big brother shot girls
With spitballs and rubber bands.

I loved to play marbles
And read comic books.
As a girl I should have
Been learning to cook.

But you only get to be a child
Once in your life.
Time passed quickly
And I became a wife.

It's now in the nineties,
And on the first day of May,
I called my mother and asked to go barefoot.
She said "Okay."

Remembering

When folks walked most places,
They knew all their neighbors.
Children played street games.
Parents knew where their teens were.

Families walked to church.
Children walked to school.
On a hot summer day,
A hosepipe kept them cool.

While visiting on the porch,
Surrounded by pretty flower pots,
The mamas were discussing
Whose children were going to tie the knot.

Thoughts and opinions were shared
While making ice cream in a churn.
A lot was being done
As each one took his turn.

Summer Nights and Lightnin' Bugs

Back before the air conditioner,
Summer nights were hot.
I'd often end up on the porch
To sleep in a cooler spot.

I watched the lightnin' bugs
I had caught and put in a jar.
Then I fell off to sleep,
Dreaming I was a movie star.

When I awoke, I caught a June bug
And tied one leg with string.
It then would fly at my control
Until I released the poor wretched thing.

Sometimes I spent the night with friends,
And we had pillow fights.
The next day we played a game
Called "One, Two, Three Red Light."

I liked to wish upon a star
And search for the man in the moon.
I played my ukulele
And sang a catchy tune.

It was fun reading with a flashlight
Hidden under the sheet.
Mayonnaise sandwiches, except for the crumbs,
Made it all seem so complete.

Though summer nights were often hot,
And mosquito bites were sprayed with Bactine;
Watching lightnin' bugs in a jar
Made life seem so serene.

11

A Hot Water Bottle On A Cold Winter Night

A hot water bottle
On a cold winter night
Felt good to the feet
After no firelight.

If you ever forgot
Your hot water bottle,
You learned the next night
To remember and not dawdle.

The quilts that Granny made
Were piled quite high;
With them and your water bottle,
You were ready for shut eye.

Sometimes you slept with
Bobby pins in your hair;
Hoping no one saw
And thought you a nightmare.

I miss my hot water bottle
And the days of old;
When on a cold winter night
My feet are ice cold.

The Path To Granny's House

The path to Granny's house
Was a much shorter way.
Granny was one street over.
I went most everyday.

There was an old rooster
That lived next door.
He chased me down the path
And pecked my feet sore.

Now that old rooster
Had pecked many more,
Until it pecked its owner,
He had chosen to ignore.

He then took that old rooster.
Its neck he did wring.
His wife made chicken and dumplings,
And my heart did sing.

Grandmother's Sewing

I used to watch my grandmother
Sew at her Singer machine.
She would keep me occupied
With a button on a string.

She made collars for my sweaters
And full poodle skirts.
I stayed very skinny;
Despite eating rich desserts.

I wore three or four crinolines
And my birthstone ring.
My petticoats filled
The whole porch swing.

I liked to wear dungarees,
But not to school.
That's where you wore dresses,
And learned the golden rule.

Grandpa's Farm

When I visited
My Grandfather's farm,
I found there
A certain charm.

Well water was brought in
And put in a pail.
A dipper used by all
Was hung on a nail.

Real butter was poured
Into a mold.
With a little color added,
It looked like gold.

The old wood stove
Cooked good "streak-o-lean."
There were odd-looking rollers
On the washing machine.

Outside, a little house
Had a seat with two round holes.
It seemed ever so often,
Someone took a little stroll.

Living on my grandpa's farm
May have made some people yearn
To have things a little easier
And live more modern.

Memory Lane

I like to stroll
Down memory lane,
Searching back deep
Within my brain.

I remember times with mother
On her knees using Johnson wax
As I sat at the table
Looking for the prize in my Cracker Jacks.

Mother would fix cornbread
And plain tomato soup,
Then send me out to play
With my hula hoop.

Sometimes I played with friends
A game called "Leap Frog."
I enjoyed Daddy getting us together
To order from Sears Roebuck Catalog.

Life was full,
With many things being imaginary,
Especially after losing a tooth
To be picked up by the tooth fairy.

It was a time
When we didn't forget to say grace.
We were thankful our saddle oxfords
Had new shoelace.

I liked to read fairy tales
And Aesop's Fables.
I probably should have
Read more about Cain and Abel.

During war time,
You heard a lot about Uncle Sam;
But you weren't on the road so much
Caught up in a traffic jam.

You didn't hear about
A place called Amsterdam.
You thought being a long way off
Was being in Birmingham.

At Thanksgiving you hoped
You would get the pulley bone
And play with cousins
A game of Jack Stones.

When you got older,
You could go to the skating rink
And write with a fountain pen
That you dipped in ink.

You could sit
With a boy on a hay ride.
You could watch a scary movie
About Dr. Jekyll and Mr. Hyde.

I like to stroll
Down memory lane,
Searching back deep
Within my brain.

Yesterday

The youngest and oldest
Child who lives today
Can still enjoy
The toys and games of yesterday.

We took broom handles
And small blocks of wood
To make stilts called Tom Walkers,
And on them we stood.

It was fun making flip books,
With pictures that moved.
As we grew older,
Our drawings improved.

It was fun playing chop sticks
With a partner on the piano;
Or better still,
Was walking the dog with a yo-yo.

If you were still very young,
You could ride piggy back.
If you were older, you could
Sing a song called Yakkity-Yak.

You could play "Step on the Crack"
Out on the sidewalk
Or play an inside game
And land on Boardwalk.

If you had string,
You could make Jacob's ladder
Or read about Alice in Wonderland
And the strange Mad Hatter.

A famous person back then
Was a child named Shirley Temple.
She played the part of "Heidi"
And showed her dimples.

It was fun going to school,
And being in a spelling bee.
You didn't want to misspell
The longest word, Mississippi.

Not all was fun and games.
We still had our chores
Of packing Red Cross boxes and praying
There would soon be no more wars.

House Calls

They said I had to go to school.
It wasn't time to go.
The school was just across the street.
I walked very slow.

The doctor was making a house call.
There was going to be a blessed event.
I really wanted to stay at home,
But I didn't cause an argument.

When I came in for lunch,
I looked in the bassinet.
There I saw my little sister.
I will never forget.

I grew up and married.
My sister visited me.
I had gone to the hospital,
To have a baby.

Now some old ways are tried again,
But I don't believe I ever recall
Anything changing back as drastically
As doctors making house calls.

Decision Time

I was saved at twelve
In the church down the street.
On alternate Sundays
The Methodists and Baptists would meet.

We would sing praises
Of Amazing Grace.
We were not running
And playing chase.

The fun we were having
Would far exceed
Anything else that could happen;
Everyone agreed.

What we were learning
Would affect the rest of our life-
Even in choosing a husband
And becoming a wife.

Life is not perfect
And all without pain;
But at the end of time,
There will be much to gain.

I hope I will fulfill
What God had in mind
When he created me
And my purpose assigned.

Paper Dolls And Sears Roebuck Catalog

The old Sears Roebuck catalog
Takes me down memory lane.
My cousin and I spent hours
Making paper dolls that entertained.

We would take our scissors
And the old discarded book,
Then go up in the attic,
Sit down, and take a look.

You could have more dolls
If you cut out your own.
You didn't have to spend money.
None of them were clones.

We would cut out our dolls
And paste them to cardboard
While my aunt was tending
Real clothes on the old washboard.

It wasn't very hard
Finding them something to wear.
We would alter paper dresses
As we spent hours upstairs.

Moving Day

On moving day
We didn't go far.
It was just down the street.
We didn't need a car.

My daddy worked
In the cotton mill.
He was closer to work,
When we moved down the hill.

Our new house
Had a skeleton key.
It didn't really matter
For neighbors were family.

Milk was put on the steps
By the milkman;
While mother cooked
In her iron frying pan.

I went across the street
When it was time for school.
There my teachers,
Taught me the golden rule.

Next to the school
Was a fine clinic.
A nurse lived there.
She helped the sick.

I could still walk up the street
When I needed the store.
In my new house,
We had an underpinned floor.

It would be nice today
Not to need a car-
For school, church, and work
Not to be far.

Growing Up In The Fifties

It was really nice
Growing up in the fifties.
There were many things to do.
Life was quite nifty.

On a hot summer night,
It was fun going to a drive-in movie.
Adjusting the sound of the speaker
On your car window was groovy.

You could gaze at the stars
Way up in the sky.
If you were lucky,
The cartoon would be about a sailor named Popeye.

The music was great.
You could do the stroll.
The jukebox always had
Some new rock and roll.

The soda jerk
Made good cherry coke floats.
If you had a boy friend,
You could pass him a love note.

It was always fun
Roasting wieners and marshmallows
And holding hands
With your favorite fellow.

For those who had television,
There was Captain Kangaroo.
There was still a respect
For the red, white, and blue.

There were crinolines, poodle skirts,
And rolled up dungarees.
There might even be
Some rare teenager with their own car keys.

Drive-in restaurants
Were a great place to eat.
Food was brought to your car
Without you leaving your seat.

It was relaxing just to sit
Out on the porch and swing.
You could sit and think,
Or you could do nothing.

It was really nice
Growing up in the fifties.
There were many things to do.
Life was quite nifty.

Home Remedies And Other Cures

Back before the specialists,
Home remedies were the thing.
A little bit of tobacco
Was great for a bee sting.

Honey and whiskey
Mixed in a spoon
Was sure to make you feel better
Very very soon.

You might buy some castor oil
Or a bottle of Hadacol.
One or the other
Was sure to be a cure-all.

Sometimes you got a mustard poultice
Slapped upon your chest.
Your dear ole granny
Said that was for the best.

Remember when using home remedies,
There's no greater wealth
Than taking care of yourself
And keeping up your health.

A Ball Of String And A Well Built Kite

A big ball of string
And a well built kite
Can turn a dull day
Into one that is bright.

Some scraps from Granny's sewing basket
For making a tail;
A nice little breeze
And you're ready to sail.

Just give a little string
A delicate jerk.
Then watch your kite
Do all the work.

Look to the heavens
With the clouds floating by.
Enjoy the pull of your kite
And maybe a beautiful butterfly.

Blackberry Picking

Blackberry picking is fun
Except for the chiggers.
Blueberries are okay,
But blackberries are bigger.

You have to watch for the flowers
That will mark your spot.
Then when the berries come,
You can pick and swat.

Swatting at the chiggers
Is not the fun part,
But you forget all that
When mama serves you a blackberry tart.

You mustn't pick too early
When the berries are red.
Be careful of the thorns;
They can cause bloodshed.

A nice hot cobbler
Is a rewarding treat.
Topped with vanilla ice cream
Makes it all complete.

The Watermelon Patch

Now I don't know for sure,
But I've been told
That many years ago
Two cousins took a stroll.

They had a taste for watermelon
And went to raid a patch.
They both got away with some
Without either getting a scratch.

Both felt somewhat guilty-
Afraid of being caught.
They decided next time
Their melons should be store bought.

One cousin claims they stole.
The other says not true.
She claims it was their grandfather's patch
The two were going through.

So whether the cousins stole the melons
Or committed a childhood prank,
After fifty years or so,
They shouldn't have to walk the plank.

An Ode To Ole Butch

Ole Butch was a mongrel,
But he made his mark.
He reigned the neighborhood
Like a grand monarch.

Daddy brought him home
When he was just a pup.
He stuck around
Until he was all grown up.

He was part bulldog,
But he had a long tail.
If a cat got out,
It was sure to ail.

Cats had better stay in
Instead of smelling for rats.
Because with Butch around,
They were sure to go splat.

Ole Butch would walk
Up and down the street
Like a policeman
Patrolling on his beat.

Once he pulled my crinolines
Off the clothesline.
If mother had caught him
He'd have been a dead canine.

We had worked all day
Getting me ready for a banquet.
That ole dog
Put us both in a sweat.

We put glasses on Butch
Then took his picture.
I won't say it helped his looks.
He was certainly no emperor.

When racing him home from Granny's
Over on the next street;
Ole Butch would take a short-cut
And would always beat.

Butch fought many battles
Before dying in his sleep.
Even I had a hard time
Trying not to weep.

More than thirty years have passed
Since ole Butch made his mark;
But in my memories,
I still hear him bark.

Bennett's Store

I miss Bennett's Store
At the top of the street.
It wasn't very far.
It had lots to eat.

There were moon pies, big pickles,
And fresh loaf bread.
If mother needed any,
There were spools of thread.

I loved the big jars
With all kinds of candy.
For a little girl's sweet tooth,
Bennett's Store was real handy.

My candy was put
In a small brown sack.
I didn't need much,
Cause tomorrow I'd go back.

On the way home,
I would rest on the curb.
People would wave and say,
"She belongs to Inez and Herb."

Times Change

Times have changed.
The cotton mill has shut its doors.
Even the old village
Isn't the same anymore.

Many have died.
Others have moved away.
There's now only a handful
Of those who decided to stay.

The store up the street
Is nailed up with boards.
I wonder what relics
Within those walls are stored.

The school in the mill village
Burned to the ground.
It would seem everything
Has changed all around.

It could be bad
Holding on to the past,
But we can take the values taught
And make them last.

Mud Pies And Hot Biscuits

I wonder if I could make better hot biscuits
If I had made more mud pies.
My mother dressed me in crisp pinafores.
She wanted me to stay nice, clean, and dry.

When I visited with my cousins,
We would make mud pies for my aunt.
She would dress us in something old
And never say you can't.

Now I know my mother loved me.
She just liked to keep me clean,
But it would have been nice,
Jumping in mud puddles before I reached my teens.

Today I like things kept in order.
I like them spic and span.
My cousins make nice hot biscuits.
My married daughter is going to teach me so I can.

Grandmama's Corner

Up the stairs
And a turn to the right
Is a place prepared
For a child's delight.

It is Grandmama's Corner,
Full of special toys
For all different ages
Of children to enjoy.

Grandmama's Corner
Is a good corner to be in.
The grandchildren seem
To want to come back, again and again.

There's a rocky horse, teddy bear,
And a jack in the box,
An aunt's little rocking chair,
And lots of blocks.

There's Shirley Temple paper dolls,
And an old Light Bright.
There's enough to do
If you spend the night.

There's high heels, pocketbooks,
And earbobs for dress up.
Even Grandmama's there
If you need to cuddle up.

There's checkers, puzzles,
And games to play.
You could live up there
And be a castaway.

Pictures

My mother had my picture made
Each and every year.
I tried to stop this practice,
But she said no, loud and clear.

Because I am a teacher,
I continue to sit and pose-
Although I get depressed
When every wrinkle shows.

My husband says,"What's wrong?
It looks just like you."
Of course, he's right.
I can't even change my hairdo.

Now my school is involved.
They have come up with a thought.
They ask me to go back in time
And bring in a baby snapshot.

This may not be so bad-
To appear so young and new.
I might even enjoy being in a book
And looking at all the "Who's Who."

Clothes On The Line

When I first married,
I hung my clothes on a line.
They blew in the breeze
And the warm sunshine.

Today I have a dryer.
Life moves at a faster pace.
I miss the cool fresh sheets
In which I use to bury my face.

I think when I retire,
I'll go back to the old way.
While I'm outside,
I may see a blue jay.

The School Bus Doesn't Stop Here Anymore

The school bus doesn't stop here anymore.
The kids are all gone.
Now the bus passes on by.
The kids have kids of their own.

It seems only yesterday
The first of my three started that ride.
The third kept going
After the first two became brides.

Even an exchange student
Rode that yellow bus, making it four.
She, too, grew up and went back home.
Now the school bus doesn't stop here anymore.

Once Upon A Childhood

Once upon a childhood
A long time ago,
I had a young cousin.
We ran to and fro.

She had a little sister,
Whom we did upset.
Often many times
We caused her to fret.

We were young children
And only meant to tease;
But my younger cousin,
Wasn't very pleased.

We would hide in the car
And be rather mean.
Now we are all three grandmothers,
But we still like to scheme.

Dreams

When I was a little girl,
I liked to sit and dream
Of all the many places
I had never seen.

I would sit for many hours
All curled up in my chair.
I'd read books of many lands.
I pretended that I was there.

Now I like to travel
And see all I can.
I like to take my maps
And make my many plans.

Vacations

Vacations aren't a luxury.
They're a necessary break.
Sometimes it's important
To go to the other side of the lake.

Jesus saw the importance
Of going to the other side.
It doesn't have to take great wealth.
It may be a short ride.

As a child I went to the beach.
My family stayed three or four days.
It didn't have to be that long
For the memories we made.

After I got married,
My husband and I continued this.
Now after each trip,
We sit back and reminisce.

Raising a family can be expensive.
Money can be tight as I recall,
But a vacation can be one long day
Picnicking by a peaceful waterfall.

Rock City

When I was just a kid,
Trips seemed very long.
The aunts, uncles, and cousins traveled together-
Feeling a bond, that we belonged.

One summer we headed to Tennessee
To a place called Rock City.
It was a place we had not been,
And we heard it was real pretty.

"See Rock City" was written on roof tops
All along the way.
One uncle drove so slow
We'd pull off and wait for him, what seemed all day.

Another didn't like to travel through cities;
He would go another way.
Often we had to wait
Because he went astray.

When we arrived, we bought things that said
"See Rock City" and other souvenirs.
Then we got our caravan together
And headed home like pioneers.

St. Augustine

There is a town in Florida
Named St. Augustine.
I lived there in the seventies.
It was very serene.

I would take my three
Little girls to the beach
Where the ocean waters
To the sky would reach.

We would play all day
And bask in the sun.
Then we returned home
When their daddy's work was done.

It was fun going across
The Bridge of Lions.
I didn't need to go to Hawaii
And be an Hawaiian.

I loved to visit the fort
And the oldest House.
I enjoyed walking through town
At night with my spouse.

The horse-drawn buggies
Would plod down the street.
The light from the lighthouse
Made it all complete.

I'm so glad I lived
Near Matanzas Bay,
Even though after two years,
I moved away.

My husband and I still cherish
The friends that we made.
The bonds are still there
After more than two decades.

St. Augustine is still
A big part of my life;
A memory to draw from
When the day has been a strife.

The Mighty Ocean

I love the mighty ocean.
I like to jump the waves.
Upon the passing of the years,
I don't feel quite as brave.

I still enjoy walking
And feeling the pulling tide,
And seeing the little sandpipers,
Racing by my side.

Oh, the mighty ocean!
It swells with great strength.
No one can measure
Its magnificent length.

I love to feel the sand,
Warm between my toes.
It also warms my heart
And makes it all aglow.

The seagulls add their music
As they fly overhead.
It doesn't take a morsel of food
To make me feel well fed.

The great mighty ocean
Has always been my friend-
Another one of God's gifts
That's hard to comprehend.

The Other Side Of The Clouds

The other side of the clouds
Was a beautiful sight.
I flew to Gothenburg, Sweden,
During both day and night.

It was my first time to fly
And to be on that side.
It was so awesome,
I almost cried.

The clouds looked
Like huge glaciers of ice.
I didn't know God had created
Such a paradise.

The clouds looked like ice,
But they didn't look cold.
They were surrounded by a sea of blue-
A sight to behold.

How could anyone not believe
In the God of all creation
After being given
Such an inspiration!

Whale Watching

I just went whale watching
Way up in Maine.
I enjoyed my trip,
And the New England terrain.

To see the whales,
I had to sail out to sea.
I thought the trip
Would be fun and carefree.

The guide was fair
And tried to inform,
But I didn't really think
There would be a storm.

It was mid evening
When we left the bay.
It seemed like
A nice way to spend the day.

At first I enjoyed
Riding the tide.
Then the waves
Became more magnified.

People on deck
Wished for more protected waters.
I too hoped to make it back
To play with my granddaughters.

Because of the storm,
I saw neither whale nor shark.
I was just glad I made it back,
To Acadia Park.

Now, there's more than whale watching
When you go to Maine.
Just remember the old saying,
"No pain, no gain."

My Husband

My husband is a Christian.
He has a special gift.
He encourages me and others.
Our spirits he uplifts.

He knows how to listen,
Which is a long-lost art.
I'm glad God gave me such a friend
To love with all my heart.

I met him in my youth.
We've shared many years.
He's the same wherever he is.
He is never insincere.

He is a faithful husband,
A loving daddy too.
He's there for his children,
And will do what he can do.

I'm thankful I've been granted
Such a wonderful man
To walk with me throughout this life
And be there to hold my hand.

A Special Lady

There is a special lady.
She means a lot to me.
When I was very little,
She held me on her knee.

I always liked to tease her.
One day I locked her out.
She went around to the other door
And hoped I wasn't about.

She would sit up with me at night
When I was very sick.
She didn't leave my side
Until a spell with asthma I had licked.

This lady kept many children
In her home, year after year,
To send me to college,
Although she wanted me near.

She used to deliver Home Life Magazines
To shut-ins and many others.
I am very glad to claim this wonderful lady.
She is my precious mother.

A Special Man

My daddy is a special man.
His age is seventy-seven.
The neatest thing about him
Is he will meet me up in heaven.

He often times forgets his age
And thinks he is nineteen.
Way down deep inside of me,
I really think that's keen.

Sometimes he worries me
When he doesn't behave.
Three years ago, he took me to Myrtle Beach,
And we jumped lots of waves.

My daddy loves the game of golf.
It's hard to tie him down.
At least twice a week,
To Hayesville, N.C., he is bound.

Daddy teaches Sunday School.
He really loves his class.
He teaches a group of girls-
The oldest an eighty-six-year-old lass.

Daughters

A daughter was born.
She was mine and my husband's first.
We had a new role in life
That never had been rehearsed.

She entered this world
In nineteen sixty-three.
She was a wonderful addition
To our family tree.

As a small child
She had a pretend friend.
We had to be careful
And try to comprehend.

She grew up fast.
She gave us pride.
With God's help,
We tried to guide.

We watched her leave
And go to college.
There she gained
More wisdom and knowledge.

It was hard for us
When she went on a mission trip,
But we knew she would look
To God for leadership.

Nineteen sixty-six was a wonderful year.
Our next daughter made her big premier.

Her daddy and I cherished her.
We watched her grow.
We were very proud
When she played the piano.

God gave her the talent of a beautiful voice.
Whenever she sang, we did rejoice.
Her music seemed more important than food.
It always seemed to help, no matter the mood.

When our third was born, it was a blessed event.
From the beginning, she wanted to be independent.
She thought she was grown at the age of three.
We tried to convey she wasn't and keep her sugar free.

I remember the year
She wanted an Atari.
She worked long and hard.
At least it wasn't a Ferrari.

We were proud
That she was somewhat aggressive.
We just didn't want it
To be too excessive.

Having daughters has given
My husband and me insight
Of how God can take a life
And make it just right.

Now they are all mothers
With daughters of their own.
They will learn too soon
They are only on loan.

A Good Leader

I appreciate my youth leader's dedication-
The time she gave to the youth.
She had us memorize scripture
And know God's word as truth.

We didn't just play and forget our purpose
When we went to God's church.
She taught us that, while there,
His word we were to search.

We had fun and games.
She planned for youth fellowship.
But also had Bible sword drills
And became fast through her leadership.

At the end of each fellowship,
We held hands and sang "Bless Be The Tie That Binds."
Then she had each of us quote
A different verse of scripture that came to our minds.

Many years have passed.
It isn't as easy to memorize.
I'm thankful for my stored verses
And a leader that was so wise.

I appreciate my youth leader, my parents,
And others that taught me God's word.
There is nothing more important,
That could ever be heard.

Friends

There are two ladies
Who are very best friends.
They couldn't be closer
If God had made them kin.

These two women are named
Inez and Elmo.
Each and every Wednesday
Bargain hunting they go.

One is seventy-five.
The other is eighty-six.
It doesn't take much
For them to get their kicks.

They both like cream gravy
And delicious butter beans;
But they also watch their figures,
So they don't have tight seams.

These two friends
Can have a ball,
Simply by walking
Through the shopping mall.

There's never a cross word
Between these two.
They never run out
Of something to do.

The friendship between them
Goes back very far.
It goes back before
The Second World War.

They keep each other's secrets
And always agree
Someone's friend
Is a special thing to be.

Changes

Sometimes obstacles
May block our passage;
But if we seek another way,
It could be to our advantage.

We may have to change
And reroute for awhile.
It may be hard to understand,
Having to take the extra mile.

There can be beauty in new routes,
Though they may take longer.
God could use them
To make us grow stronger.

New experiences can make
Life more interesting.
What first seemed a burden
Could become a blessing.

So when routes in our life
Make a sudden change;
Remember our vision is limited,
But God's view is long range.

The Dogwood

There once was a beautiful Dogwood tree
In the backyard.
It was a lovely sight to view
Until weather battered and scarred.

It had lifted its adorned branches
Up to the sky;
As one of God's pieces of work,
It tried to exemplify.

As time went by,
Its limbs did slump.
The tree was cut down
And became a stump.

Two years have past
And now it's spring.
Out of that old stump
Comes a wonderful thing.

New life is growing.
Blossomed branches uplift.
God again is giving
Us a glorious gift.

In Different Shoes

As we travel this life through,
We walk with feet in different shoes.
Many miles along the way,
May the Lord guide each day.

Often skies are gray or blue,
As we walk in different shoes.
May we seek our Savior's will
In a worship time that's still.

Lord help us not to hurt or bruise,
As we walk in different shoes;
But may we each and everyone
Remember daily what You have done.

Life Is A Gift

Life is a gift
We don't need to waste.
Responsibilities on each of us
Have been placed.

As long as we're here,
There is a job to do.
We need to remember our Maker
And to Him be true.

If we are God's children,
Our lives will never end.
We need to search daily
For how our lives we spend.

Lord, help us seek Your way-
Not go out on our own.
May You be pleased with us
And our timepieces You have loaned.